HIDEAWAY HOUSE

ISBN 1 85854 269 3
© Brimax Books Ltd 1995. All rights reserved.
Published by Brimax Books Ltd, Newmarket, England CB8 7AU 1995.
Printed in Dubai.

HIDEAWAY HOUSE

BY
GILL DAVIES
ILLUSTRATED BY
ERIC KINCAID

Brimax · Newmarket · England

Monty Mouse Finds a House

Hideaway House was sad. No one had lived there for a long time; and although there were lots of other buildings around, the old gabled house lay lost and forgotten behind its overgrown garden, all alone in the middle of town.

Monty Mouse was playing hide and seek when he discovered Hideaway House. He was scrambling between tall, rusty railings to hide from Jemima, Sammy, and Mischief when he spotted a path leading beyond the tangle of bushes. At the end of the path stood Hideaway House.

Monty slipped inside the broken door, and there the other little mice found him some minutes later. Sunlight filtered through the cobwebbed windows and a haze of dust twisted and danced in the shafts of light. The room was empty except for an old dresser and a rocking chair.

Monty, who liked exploring, scampered across the floor, leaving a trail of tiny paw prints behind him in the dust.

The other mice followed. At the end of the kitchen was a half-open door. Beyond that door was a pantry.

"Goodness!" said Monty.

"Wow!" said Sammy.

"Look at all that food!" said Mischief and Jemima together.

The pantry was full. It had a wide marble top and deep wooden shelves from floor to ceiling. And on every shelf there were jars and packets and tins and bags and bottles.

"Fancy leaving so much behind," said Monty. "They must have left in a real hurry."

"There is sugar up here," called Jemima, running along the shelf, "and raisins and cookies!"

"This," remarked Sammy some time later between mouthfuls of cookie, "would be a very wonderful place to live. I'm very glad you found Hideaway House, Monty."

"And me," said Jemima, nibbling a date.

"And me," said Mischief, munching spaghetti.

When they had eaten, ready to burst, the little mice hurried back to Downbeat Hotel, where they lived under the floorboards with Pa and Ma Whiskers.

"One at a time, one at a time," said Pa Whiskers, as the excited mice all tried to talk at once about sugar and raisins and cookies.

"Please," the little mice chorused, "please can we go and live there?"

"We'll have to see," said Pa Whiskers.

The next morning the whole family set off together up the steep, grassy slope to where Hideaway House was waiting for them.

Pa and Ma Whiskers liked it very much.

"We need a change," said Ma Whiskers. "The house needs a good scrub but it's really grand and the garden is wonderful!"

She was staring at a strawberry plant which was weighed down with all the fruit growing on it. Pa was exploring the vegetable patch.

"Right!" announced Pa. "The Whisker family will move. Let's go and pack!"

So the next day the mice took all their belongings up the steep slope to Hideaway House. The beetles from Downbeat Hotel took turns pulling Pa's matchstick cart while the mouse family carried overflowing bags and suitcases.

As soon as they arrived Monty set off to explore. He scrambled up the steep staircase.

"You are a real adventurer, Monty!" Ma called out after him. "I feel much safer on the ground floor. Please be careful!"

Monty spent the whole afternoon pattering along corridors and climbing up and down stairs. Soon he had peeked into every empty room – from the cool, dark cellar to the hot, dusty attic.

It was a wonderful house, full of interesting corners, with windows that looked out over the tangled garden to the towering hills beyond.

"I reckon," said Pa that evening, as the family sat down to supper in the kitchen, "we could set up in business here. We could rent out the rooms upstairs. I'm sure lots of other animals would like to live here, too."

So that is what they did. They advertised in the 'Bird and Beast Gazette'. Before long there were bats in the belfry, an owl in the top bedroom and a large toad happily settled into the ornate old bath tub. All the animals liked the house because it was so secret and hidden away.

At last Hideaway House was no longer sad and lonely. In fact it was the happiest house in town.

———— • ————

Monty Mouse Finds a Ghost

It was a warm Summer night when Monty Mouse first met the ghost. The garden of Hideaway House was full of the sweet smell of honeysuckle. Monty had popped out for a moment or two to breathe in the evening air.

"I like the night time in the garden," he said to the crickets singing in the grass.

"What are you up to, Monty?" called Ma Mouse from the kitchen door. "Are you alright?"

"Of course I am, Ma," answered Monty. "I've just come out to look at the lights. You can see the town from here, all busy and sparkling."

"Don't get cold," said Ma. "And mind the owls don't eat you."

Eric Kincaid

Monty wasn't frightened. He had helped Sebastian the Barn Owl move into the best bedroom of Hideaway House. Sebastian was very happy up there. He had also promised to tell the other owls that the Whisker family must be left alone.

Betty, one of the Batty Bats from the belfry, whizzed past his head and then hung for a moment in mid air.

"Hi there, Monty," she called. "I'm off to hunt for beetles – see you soon!" – and away she zoomed.

It was then that Monty saw the ghost.

A fluttery moth on its way down the path to the railway line had just flapped into Monty's face. Monty had to rub his eyes and everything went blurred for a moment or two. He wasn't immediately sure if the white shape by the railings was real or not.

"WOOOOO!" went the shape.

"Oooooer," went Monty.

"WOOOOO!" went the shape again. It moved up the path, getting closer to Monty.

Monty discovered that his legs were walking backwards. He was still staring at the white shape which was now flying silently up the path towards him.

"STOP!" shouted Monty Mouse, sounding braver than he felt. "Stay there. Don't come any closer till you tell me who you are."

The white shape paused and then seemed to pull itself up into a long, thin column of cloud.

"I," said the shape, "am the ghost of Hideaway House ... WOOOOOO!" He looked at Monty, who was pressing his back to the wall now.

"WOO-ooo-ooo," said the ghost a little hesitantly. "WOOOOooooo! Why aren't you running away, little mouse?"

"There's no place left to run," said Monty. "Anyway," he went on, beginning to feel angry that he had been disturbed, "if you are the ghost of Hideaway House, why aren't you inside the house where you belong?"

"Because," wailed the ghost rather sadly, "someone has stolen the haunted bedroom. A big-eyed bird with ragged wings is sitting on the bedpost all the time. There are animals in every room and there's nowhere left for a ghost to unwind in peace."

"Oh dear!" said Monty. "I think that may be my fault. I told Sebastian the Barn Owl to choose the best room. I had no idea it was haunted."

"Well, it isn't anymore," said the ghost, rather crossly. "I've been driven out to haunt the garden, and I don't like it at all. It's cold out here, and no one takes any notice of me at all."

Then he began to cry. He huddled up into a tight ball and let the tears roll down his face and fall on to the path.

"I think," said Monty, "that you had better come inside with me and we'll see what we can do."

So he led the sobbing ghost back in through the door to the kitchen where Ma Mouse was just putting a delicious hot apple pie on to the table.

"Hello," said Ma. "Who is this sad fellow? Does he want a piece of pie? That might cheer him up and put some meat on his bones. He looks in need of something."

"I," said the ghost, pulling himself up again, "am the ghost of Hideaway House."

He looked at Ma Whiskers and the warm crusty pie and then he seemed to crumple down a little and become saggy at the edges. "But I must say that pie looks delicious. I haven't eaten apple pie for ages, not once since I've been dead!"

"No wonder you're so white-faced," said Ma, giving the ghost a thick wedge of pie. "There, get that down you and you'll feel much better, I'm sure."

While the ghost was busy eating, the other mice came in to peep at him, tiptoeing through the door and staring as Ma told him to help himself to a second – and then a third – fat slice of pie.

Then Monty took the ghost upstairs into the blue bedroom on the top floor.

"This can be yours," he said. "Mole moved into the cellar last week, so this is a spare."

"Oh, thank you-oooooo," said the ghost. "It's lovely – beautiful pale blue walls to glide through and a view of the railway line. I'm sure I shall be very comfortable here."

And so he was. He upset new arrivals occasionally by haunting them when they weren't expecting it, but the animals in Hideaway House soon discovered he was a dear old ghost. They all became enormously fond of him, almost as fond as he became of Ma Whisker's excellent apple pie.

———— • ————

The Rainy Day

Monty Mouse was bored.

Today he had planned to make a den in the garden. He had found the perfect spot - a nice dry corner hidden between the plant pots and overhung with a green roof of ivy. He had been looking forward to sorting it out this morning but now he was stuck indoors.

It was raining. It was raining very hard. The gutters of Hideaway House streamed with water that gushed over in places like a waterfall. Rain lashed the windows and bounced off the garden path. It was very, very wet.

"Staring at it won't bring the sunshine out," said Pa Whiskers, who was putting cookies into bags ready for market.

"Why don't you go and play with the others?" said Ma, stirring popcorn.

Jemima, Sammy, and Mischief were taking turns trying to balance on a rolling cork.

But Monty didn't want to. He was fed up.

"I can't even talk to the other animals," he grumbled.

Mole was in bed with a bad cold. Sebastian Owl and the Batty Bats were fast asleep. The Squirrels had gone to visit their relatives in the park, and Timothy Toad was outside hopping about in the wet grass, enjoying the rain.

"What about Racer Rat?" suggested Ma Whiskers. "He might be lonely up in the attic."

"That's a good idea," said Monty, cheering up. "I'd forgotten about Racer."

He jumped down from the window sill and set off immediately on the long climb to the top of the house.

When he was about halfway there, the ghost of Hideaway House heard Monty scampering along and came out to see him.

"Where are yoooouuu off tooooooo, Monty?" he asked.

"I'm going to call on Racer Rat in the attic," said Monty.

"Can I come toooooo?" pleaded the ghost.

"Of course you can," said Monty.

They reached the top of the house in no time at all, for the ghost just flew up the stairs, carrying Monty with him.

A ladder led up from the top landing to a neat little hole in the ceiling.

Racer Rat heard them coming and was peeping down at them over the edge of the hole.

"Watch out, Racer," warned the ghost, sweeping upwards. He pulled himself into a long thin shape and then oozed through the hole, taking Monty with him.

Racer Rat was a very jolly fellow, always laughing and busy and rushing about.

"Bless me," he cried. "It's jolly good to see you two on such a morning. It's raining so much, I can't hear myself think today."

The rain was pounding loudly on the attic roof as Racer Rat bustled about to fetch cups and saucers and a plate of cheese.

"Now," he said, "I can't tell you how pleasant it is to have visitors. It's such a long journey up here that I think you fellows downstairs forget about me sometimes."

The attic was a lovely, jumbly sort of place with boxes and books, newspapers and picture frames, broken furniture, bags of old clothes, two sewing machines, and a chest stuffed full of letters.

Racer lived in the sunniest corner below a dusty skylight where his friend, Legs the Spider, kept watch on the outside world and told Racer what was going on.

"Still pouring down," said Legs, rather unnecessarily, as the noise of the rain drumming on the roof was even louder than before.

After they had drunk their sweet apple tea, Racer scampered about excitedly. He was thrilled to have a chance to show them his stamp collection and the photographs of his relatives downtown. He showed them how he had slung his hammock over the hot water pipe where it was really warm.

"I have to be careful that I don't topple out, though," he said laughing. "I might singe my whiskers!"

Time flew by, until suddenly Legs the Spider span around in his web and called out cheerily, "Hey there, the rain has stopped. I can see some blue sky and Ma Whiskers has come out with the washing."

"Yippee!" said Monty. "Now I can make my den."

"Off you go," said Racer. "But do come and see me again soon. It cheers a fellow up to see his friends, don't you know."

So the ghost and Monty Mouse said goodbye and flew downstairs.

Monty had a lovely afternoon. He was busy in his den between the flower pots, under the ivy roof. But every now and then he popped out into the open to wave to the little attic skylight, to Legs the Spider and Racer Rat, high in their snug little home.

"How lucky I am," he said to himself, "to have such good friends – especially on a rainy day."

———— • ————

Jim Fox the Tramp

It was snowing the day Jim Fox arrived.

The previous night the wind had whistled and whined and blown very cold. "It could almost cut you in half," Ma Whiskers said.

But that morning when the mice awoke, there was a strange silence. Monty sat up in bed, wondering why his room was dark. Then he saw the snow piled high against the window.

Monty was very excited. He gobbled his breakfast and left half of his bread. Then he pulled on his boots and went outside.

The garden of Hideaway House was covered in a thick white blanket of snow. Huge drifts hid the plants and the path and leaned against the railings.

Soon Pa came out with a shovel to clear a path. Mischief and Sammy joined Monty and threw snowballs. Jemima built a snowmouse.

It was then that Ma screamed.

"Whatever's the matter?" cried Pa, throwing down his shovel and rushing inside without stopping to take off his boots. The other mice dashed behind him, leaving a snowy trail on the floor.

Ma was on the front porch with a brush in her hand, ready to sweep the step clear of snow. She was standing absolutely still, white as a sheet, with her tiny fist pushed into her mouth. She looked terrified.

Towering above her, slumped asleep in the porch and snoring loudly, was Jim Fox the tramp.

All the animals in Hideaway House had heard Ma's piercing scream. Soon Timothy Toad, Mole, and then Sebastian Owl and Betty Bat, rubbing their eyes clear of sleep, were squashed into the porch doorway peering at Jim Fox.

"That's it!" said Pa. "The last thing we want here is a fox!"

"Perhaps he won't stay," suggested Monty. "Perhaps he's just come in out of the cold."

"He'll stay," said Sebastian Barn Owl, "at least until Spring, now he's found a safe, warm spot."

Jim Fox gave a sudden snort in his sleep and Ma almost screamed again. Pa held her tight until she stopped shaking and then led her away to sit down while they decided what to do.

The other animals tiptoed into the dining room to discuss the problem, but Monty stayed behind to keep watch for a minute.

In the excitement, everyone had forgotten about the ghost of Hideaway House. He had heard Ma Whiskers' scream and then the rush of animals to the porch. Then there was silence, then whispers, and then the sudden chatter as the animals gathered to talk.

The ghost knew something must be very wrong. He hoped Ma Whiskers was all right; he had grown very fond of her, as well as of her delicious apple pie. The ghost came down to see if he could help.

Eric Kincaid

He drifted silently down the stairs and across to Monty, who was tucked behind the porch door, peering through the crack.

"Whaaaaaaaaaaat is gooooooooooing on?" inquired the ghost.

Monty jumped, startled by the ghost's sudden arrival. Then he lead him away and explained, "There's a big fox out there – a rough sort of fellow, dressed in rags. He's asleep in our porch. We don't want him here. Foxes always mean trouble and Ma's terrified of them."

The ghost looked worried for a moment, then his eyes shone with glee.

"I could haunt him if you like," he suggested. "That might scare him off."

"Would you?" said Monty. "What a terrific idea! Let's go and tell the others in the dining room."

Everyone thought that it was an excellent suggestion and that the ghost should begin immediately.

Out in the porch there was a sudden gust of wind and a fresh flurry of snow.

"AaaTISHoooo!" Jim Fox sneezed, rolled over, yawned, and sat up. He began to scratch.

"Please," begged Ma Whiskers. "Please, do go and haunt that creature immediately. My nerves can't stand much more."

"I have to prepare myself first," said the ghost.

He went out into the hallway. Then, watched by the fascinated animals, the ghost launched himself off the stairs for a few practice swooshes, whooooooooooing and wailing and pulling himself up to his greatest height.

At last the ghost was ready. He went out into the porch.

It was a little difficult to do his job properly at first. For one thing, he was used to haunting at night; and for another, the snow was so white and whirling that he could scarcely be seen.

Moreover, his wailing noises sounded much the same as the wind which was now howling even louder than he was.

Eric Kincaid

Added to these difficulties was the fact that Jim Fox had been raiding garbage bags the night before and was still half asleep.

Eventually, however, the ghost took a run up the snowy street, leapt into the air, and made a fine sweeping whoosh at Jim Fox that sent his battered top hat sailing into the snowy sky.

Jim Fox struggled to his feet and lurched off to chase his hat and to find a more peaceful spot somewhere else. He was never quite sure if he'd seen a ghost or whether it was a sudden whirl of wind and snow. However, just to be on the safe side, he decided never to go back to Hideaway House again.

All the animals were very relieved, especially Ma Whiskers, who gave the ghost a whole apple pie to himself.

The ghost was pleased too. He was happy to have helped, and it did him good to have a decent haunt now and then.

———— • ————

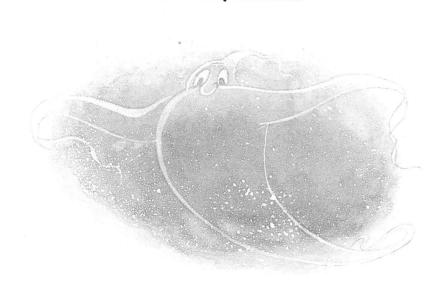